TRUE

3 Short Stories

Clean As Cotton

The Heart of Victory

Imagine

by Barbara Cutrera

Barbara Cutrera

Dedicated to my son, Joe, a smart, caring, and well-rounded human being who remains true to himself every day

Copyright 2013 by Barbara Cutrera

All Rights Reserved

Published by On My Way Up, LLC
www.onmywayuponline.com

NOTE: The characters and businesses mentioned in this work are purely fictional. Any resemblance to actual businesses or real persons, living or dead, is purely coincidental.

Cover photography by Budge Cutrera

ISBN 978-0-9858255-6-0

Clean as Cotton

Cotton Landry pulled her blonde hair back into a ponytail while she waited for the truck driver to pay her for some cigarettes. She shifted from one foot to the other as he fumbled in his pockets looking for his wallet. He eventually located a ten dollar bill and offered it to Cotton.

Acutely aware that the man was studying her a little too closely, Cotton opened the drawer of the cash register in order to get the man's change. Her face flushed as the truck driver's eyes roamed slowly over her chest, waist and hips. She focused her blue eyes on the money and gave him his bills and coins as quickly as she could before reaching back behind her to get him a pack of Camels. She passed them across the counter and forced herself to tell him to have a good day as he left the small store.

Guidry's Handi-mart and Bait Shop had been the only convenience store in the area since well before Cotton had been born. It was the hub of community life for those who lived in her little southern Louisiana town.

"Guidry's is where all the action's at," her mother, Marla, liked to say. "You want to know what's going on with anyone around these parts, then you go to Guidry's."

Cotton, always interested in what was going on anywhere, approached the owner of the store about a job the day she turned fifteen.

"You gonna go places," Robert Guidry had told her that day. "You're a real smart girl, and there ain't nobody around here who don't like you. Someday, you could be running my place."

Cotton had no intention of working at the Handimart and Bait Shop for the rest of her life. She wanted more than a dead-end job that would most certainly be accompanied by a husband who was also underemployed, several children who would be destined to the same fate, and life in a trailer or a rundown house like the one Cotton shared with her parents and grandmother.

"Hey, Cotton."

Jay Bourgeois, fellow high school student and cashier, joined her behind the counter. He was two years older than she, a senior who played on the football team and liked to go fishing with his father on the weekends. He was handsome, sweet, and going nowhere. Cotton smiled at him as she reached for her book sack.

"Happy sixteenth birthday," Jay told her. "Got any special plans?"

"Typical birthday stuff with my family."

"Have fun!" Jay called out as she left the store.

Cotton walked through the humid May night towards her house. Mosquitoes buzzed around her, and crickets serenaded her during the familiar journey home. Old Lucien's dog barked in the distance, as it always did at this time of the evening.

As she approached the little wooden house with its faded and peeling gray paint, Cotton felt both comforted and saddened. She loved the old place her grandfather had built with his own two hands for his young bride forty years earlier. It was the only home Cotton had ever known.

TRUE

The house was small and rather dilapidated but full of love and warmth. It was also a symbol of how people were content to live and die without a change in their circumstances, and Cotton supposed that was fine – for them. She had other plans.

Her dream was to become a doctor. She knew this was an unrealistic goal, despite the A+ average she'd maintained since kindergarten. Her family was dirt poor. Even with the scholarships she'd most likely be offered, there wouldn't be enough money to pay for college, let alone medical school.

An idea came to Cotton as she stood in front of the family home. She'd always been told that she was pretty, and the boys at her school certainly seemed to agree since they were constantly trying to get her to sleep with them. Men like the truck driver couldn't keep their eyes off her. Perhaps she could manage to put herself through school by being a dancer in one of the New Orleans clubs. She'd recently read an article about a girl who'd used her earnings from moonlighting as a stripper to pay her way through law school. Cotton hated the idea of letting men leer at her every night as she danced in some skimpy costume, but she was getting increasingly desperate as time passed with seemingly no other option available to her.

"Happy birthday, my baby," her father, Paul, told her as she entered the kitchen.

Paul Landry had blonde hair and blue eyes like his daughter. A good-looking man of thirty-five, he'd never worked an honest day in his life. As a provider for his family, Paul was a pathetic failure. Cotton loved him dearly.

"Your mother and MawMaw went to the store. How's my girl today?"

"Fine, Daddy," she replied, as she gave him a hug. "How was your day?"

"Last night was good for me. I won big."

Cotton nodded and put down her book sack. She got a Coke and sat at the small kitchen table. She knew how her father's stories went. She would be listening for a while.

Paul sat across from his daughter and regaled her with tales of the previous night's poker game and of how he'd won each hand. He spoke of the other men at the table and of how they'd continued to lose but had stayed for game after game in hopes of winning back their money.

It was a familiar story, one Cotton had heard her father tell repeatedly during her lifetime. Sometimes, he was the winner; sometimes he was the loser. Always, he was the consummate gambler who lived for the opportunity to best others and to surpass his own previous efforts. Results varied from day to day. No one could ever be certain whether or not Paul would bring home money or owe it to another gambling man.

It was a hard way for the Landry family to live. Cotton's mother earned little working as a cleaning woman for their church, and MawMaw Evy had been out of a job since the Dairy Queen on the highway had burned to the ground thanks to an arsonist's torch.

As her father ended his story, he asked, "Who's the best poker player in all this place?"

"You are, Daddy."

"And you're the best little girl a father could ask for. That's why I have something special for you on your birthday. There's only one condition."

Her curiosity peaked, Cotton echoed, "Condition?"

Paul nodded soberly and said, "Promise me you'll do what I ask, baby."

"I promise," she said without hesitation.

Her father left the room, returning moments later with a square box that had been awkwardly wrapped in colorful paper adorned with the words "Happy Birthday" and "Celebrate!"

"Open your present, then we'll talk."

"Shouldn't I wait for Mama and MawMaw Evy?"

He shook his head, and she carefully peeled back the tape and removed the wrapping paper. Easing the lid off the box, Cotton peered inside.

As she withdrew the small key, Cotton asked, "What do I do with it?"

"You keep it safe and hold onto it until the darkest day of your life. Then you take it to Ed Savoie, the lawyer. And don't you go telling anyone about this key or what I told you to do. That's your condition. Remember, you promised. Be a good girl and listen to your daddy."

"But –"

"Cotton Marie, you do as I say. Now, take that box and key to your room before anyone else sees them."

Although still perplexed, she thanked her father and hugged him before going to put away the mysterious present and her book sack. Not certain as to where she should hide the key, Cotton decided she would wear it on a chain around her neck so it wouldn't get misplaced or taken. Whatever it was that the key represented, it was obviously important to her father and, therefore, to her.

Six months passed. MawMaw Evy's COPD grew increasingly worse until it finally claimed her life. Although her grandmother's death greatly affected her, Cotton did *not* remove the chain that held the key from around her neck.

A few weeks later, Cotton's mother announced that she'd been having an affair with the groundskeeper of the Sunshine Estates Nursing Home. She asked Cotton to move with her to the man's trailer. When Cotton refused, her mother left without her. Cotton was profoundly disturbed but still didn't undo the clasp on the chain.

A year went by. One night when she was working late, she allowed Jay to take advantage of her in the storeroom. When it appeared that she might be pregnant, Cotton envisioned the realization of her greatest fear: a life spent with Jay working at the convenience store and raising her baby in a place where she felt there was no chance for a better future. Cotton took off the necklace.

Before she could take the key to the lawyer's office, Cotton was relieved to discover that she wasn't pregnant. She put the chain back on and kept going to school and to her job, although she made sure she never worked late with Jay again.

A week after graduating at the top of her class, Cotton came home from work to find the police chief parked in the gravel driveway that led to the house she shared with her father. She sensed instantly that Paul Landry was dead.

"We found him down by Aucoin's rice farm," the policeman told her. "We suspect it was someone he owed money to, and we'll do our best to find out who did this."

Once the police chief had gone, Cotton sat alone in the empty, run-down little house and cried. She lay awake all night. The next morning, she rose and walked to Mr. Savoie's office with the key clenched tightly in her fist.

"Your father came to me the day you were born," the lawyer told her once she was seated in front of his desk. Shaking his head, he said, "I'm sorry to hear about Paul. He had his faults, but he was a good man who'd do anything for his family and his friends."

Cotton agreed and held out the key.

"You hold it and come with me to the bank," he told her.

An hour later, Cotton stood alone in the eerie quiet of the room that held all the safe deposit boxes. The bank president had taken the key she'd proffered and used it in conjunction with one of his in order to open the little door for box G-7. Then he'd left her alone while he and Mr. Savoie went to talk in his office.

Cotton lifted the lid of the box. The first thing she saw was a handmade card she'd created with construction paper and markers for her father when she'd been five years old. Underneath the card was a picture of her taken at the hospital just after she'd been born, the wispy light blonde hair almost white in the photo. What followed were pictures of various important events in her life, ending with the graduation photo snapped only the previous week. Below that was an envelope that had "Cotton Marie Landry" written on the front.

She withdrew its contents and opened the paper with trembling hands. On it was written a sequence of numbers. It was signed *Love, Your Daddy* at the bottom.

Cotton stared at the paper for a long time. Was her father giving her some sort of code, some lucky numbers he expected her to bet on at the track, a casino, or in a card game?

She wiped at the tears on her cheeks and put everything except the paper back into the box then pocketed the key and went to find Mr. Savoie. When she located him and the bank president she held out the paper with the numbers written on it and waited.

"Your daddy did everything he could to provide for your future," Savoie declared with conviction.

"That he did," the banker agreed. "Paul sought out our help, and we were proud to give it."

"Paul knew himself all too well." Savoie cleared his throat and admitted, "The day you were born he vowed he'd do right by you."

"He did," Cotton insisted. "He loved me. He was proud of me."

Savoie concurred but insisted, "As your daddy, he knew he should do more. That's why he came to us."

"But what could you do?"

"Every time Paul won any money, he brought half of it to me," the lawyer explained. "I was charged with bringing it to the bank. I agreed to give

Paul the account number, since the account didn't have his name on it, only yours and mine. He wrote it on that piece of paper and asked that I put it in a safe deposit box. Sometimes, he'd bring me pictures he wanted to add to the box when he'd bring money. Once, he brought me that card you made for him. He said he'd been real low that day, and the card had given him hope. He said just knowing that he'd helped create someone as beautiful and smart as his Cotton gave him reason to go on."

"We were amazed that he never reneged on his vow," the banker remarked. "Gamblers don't usually have the ability to part with their money unless it's to gamble with it."

"Sometimes it'd be only a few dollars," the lawyer said. "Sometimes it'd be thousands. It added up over the last eighteen years."

Cotton dropped her eyes and stared at her hands. When she felt she could speak without crying, she asked, "How much is there?"

"One hundred eighty-three thousand one hundred dollars and seventeen cents," the bank president replied.

"Excuse me?"

"You heard him right," the lawyer said quietly. "It's all yours."

"You don't have to make any decisions today," the banker told her. "That money's not going anywhere."

But I am, Cotton thought. *I'm going away from this place. I'm going to do something with my life, something that will make my Daddy smile down from Heaven.*

Cotton soon rented out her little house and left for college in New Orleans. She went to class during the day and worked in a convenience store in the evenings. She enjoyed the time spent with her college friends but focused most of her energy on her studies.

As the years went by, Cotton had no desire to return to the little town of her birth. She married a fellow medical student and was happy in New Orleans. She would certainly have a more successful career there once she and her husband passed their medical board exams. Yet, something tugged at her conscience, and Cotton knew she had to go home at least one more time before she could determine which course her life should take.

The day after "M.D." was added to the end of her name, she decided to return to her hometown for a visit. She rose early and drove from New Orleans to her old house, which was presently not rented. During her time away, she'd paid a local handyman to fix some of the more pressing problems in the home and had also paid him to give the old structure a fresh coat of white paint.

It already looks dingy, she thought, as she stepped out of her car and walked towards the front door.

While wandering through the rooms, Cotton thought of her easy-going gambler father, her larger-than-life grandmother and of the mother she hadn't spoken to in over ten years. She emerged still uncertain about her future and drove aimlessly for over an hour, finally stopping at Guidry's Handi-mart and Bait Shop in order to get herself something cool to drink.

"Hey, Cotton!"

"Jay Bourgeois?"

"In the flesh. It's been a long time! Ed Savoie said you'd gone off to medical school. Are you a doctor now?"

"A pediatrician."

"Imagine that," he said with a grin, as he rang up her Coke. "I've got four kids of my own now. I've started taking them fishing this year. The oldest says he wants to work here with me when he turns fifteen." Handing her the change from her five dollar bill, Jay leaned forward slightly and added, "He says he wants to be the manager when I retire."

Cotton smiled and nodded before telling Jay it was wonderful to see him after so many years. She dropped her change into the tip jar before saying goodbye.

"You have to go so soon?"

"I do."

"Too bad. You know, it's a shame they never found out who killed your daddy. Mama always said Paul Landry could have done great things if he'd lived."

Her hand on the door handle, Cotton said, "He did the greatest thing of all. He gave me life."

And with those words, Cotton was free.

Barbara Cutrera

TRUE

The Heart of Victory

"I'm getting out of the spy games," Thomas Jones announced to his older brother one afternoon. "I'm done, Victor."

"Don't be stupid. You and I were groomed to do this and are better than just about everyone else in The Agency. Our parents were killed in the line of duty and wanted us to carry on in their stead. We're the big, brainy, blonde-haired brown-eyed bad ass Jones brothers. You're only thirty and have a lot of years left being on top."

"I'm tired of being on top. I'm tired of seeing what we see every day, of doing what we do. I need to be in the light for a change."

"What in the hell is that supposed to mean?"

"It means I won't kill again," Thomas answered quietly but resolutely. "I wish I'd never killed in the first place."

"What we do saves innocents."

"It's still murder, and I won't be a part of it any longer."

Victor demanded that his brother rethink his position and listen to reason.

"I'm not changing my mind," Thomas insisted. "I want to use my degree in mechanical engineering to actually work in the field. I always dreamed about that and about living in the ordinary world. I want to lead a normal life. That's something you and I have never had."

"It's a woman, isn't it? A woman has to be responsible for this ridiculousness."

"No woman," his brother declared. "Although I wouldn't mind finding some nice girl, falling in love, and having a couple of kids. You're thirty-three and have a Master's degree in economics. Don't you ever dream about doing what I plan to do?"

"No."

"Then just call me crazy."

"You're crazy," Victor snapped. "You've got it all."

"I have nothing. *You* have nothing." Taking a sip of his wine, Thomas asked, "Have you ever been in love?"

"Love is a complication we can't afford ourselves. You know that."

Thomas nodded and said, "It's lonely being judge, jury, and executioner." Rising, he repeated, "I'm done."

"You'll change your mind."

"No, but I will be in touch at some point."

Victor glanced away and said nothing. His brother was turning his back on their parents, on The Agency, and on him. He was betraying everything they'd worked for since as long as either of them could remember.

For two years Victor had no contact with Thomas. He played the spy games and lived in a sparsely-furnished apartment in D.C. when he wasn't on a job. One day he returned from an assignment in Turkey to find a wedding invitation from Thomas in his mailbox. He immediately went to the phone and called his younger brother.

"Who is she?" he demanded when Thomas answered.

"Hello to you, too."

"Well?"

Sighing, Thomas said, "Sonia's a teacher."

"Where'd you meet her?"

"The Secret Policemen's Ball."

Victor hesitated and pondered this piece of information. So, his future sister-in-law had been an operative as well. Perhaps...

"I'm still retired from my old job," Thomas said as if in answer to his brother's thoughts. "She's retired, too."

Victor grunted and decided to do his best to conceal his disappointment.

"I want you to be my Best Man, Victor."

"Sure."

Thomas paused before volunteering, "I'm really happy. Can't you try to be happy for me?"

"I still think you made a mistake two years ago."

"I did the right thing. You should try it."

"No, thanks. Just tell me when to get the tux and where to stand."

Sonia Ruslan turned out to be a tall, slim, athletically-built brunette who was currently teaching history at the high school level. As Victor stood beside his brother on the porch of an impressive plantation home and watched Sonia walk down the path between the rows of white chairs set up on the lawn, he almost laughed out loud. All of the wedding guests were under the impression that Thomas was simply a mechanical engineer, that Sonia was merely a high school teacher, and that Victor was no more than an economist. None of them suspected that the groom, bride, and the best man had been trained to investigate, to act, to kill.

A year later, Sonia gave birth to a daughter. Victor reluctantly went to the hospital to see his newborn niece. As he looked down at the tiny baby with her smooth skin, pink lips, and brown hair, Victor felt an odd sensation in his chest. She was so…alive. She was also completely defenseless against the horrors of the world.

"We want you to name her," Thomas told his brother, as Sonia and the baby slept.

"What? Why? No. She's not my kid."

Before he realized what was happening, Victor found himself against the wall. He'd never expected Thomas to come at him in anger, especially not in the same room with his wife and infant daughter.

"What do you think you're doing?" he hissed.

"I'm trying to coax you into joining the human race," his brother hissed back. "You don't have any connection to anything except your work and to me."

"That's plenty."

Thomas snorted and remarked, "Hardly. Are you capable of caring about someone else so deeply that you'd die for them?"

"What do you think I've been doing since we were kids? I care so much about every person in this country that I'd die for them. That's what people like us do. We give our lives for our nation and for those who live in it if that's what's called for."

"And lose ourselves in the process?"

Victor shook his head and said, "Stop overanalyzing me. I do my job and do it well. At the end of the day there are a few less monsters out there because of me."

"And one more piece of your soul that's been chipped away."

"Aren't you the freakin' poet?"

"Prove me wrong," Thomas challenged. Releasing the front of his brother's shirt, he ordered, "Give my daughter a name and swear that you'll be there for her. Swear to me that you won't try to turn her into what we became."

Victor stared at the baby and felt the tightening in his chest once more. He awkwardly reached forward and touched her tiny fingers with his thumb. Unable to stop himself, he gave a slight smile when she made a small noise and tried to grasp at the digit.

"I swear I'll protect her and won't try to make her into one of us," he declared with a hint of resignation in his voice. "As for naming her, what if you hate the name I pick?"

"Sonia and I want this. You'll do fine with it."

Victor studied the sleeping baby for a long time then offered, "How about Tory?"

Thomas grinned and said, "I like it. You're going to be a fantastic uncle."

Victor immediately began to receive e-mails about Tory from his brother and envelopes that held photos of the growing baby. When Thomas invited him to come for the Thanksgiving holidays, he surprised himself by readily accepting. Although he was hesitant at first about holding Tory, Victor quickly found that he enjoyed having the infant in his arms. She seemed comfortable in his embrace, and he was happy when she was nestled against him.

Over the next five years, Victor delighted in watching his niece develop from an infant into a toddler then into a preschooler and then into a kindergartener. The child was tall and lean with brown hair and eyes. Tory was quick-witted, happy, and giving. She continually brought joy to her parents, her friends, her teachers, to strangers, and to her uncle. He sent her presents from around the world and visited her whenever he wasn't on assignment. She never failed to have smiles and hugs for him, and her artwork soon decorated his apartment walls and refrigerator.

As Tory matured, she continued to have an almost ethereal aura of well-being surrounding her. The fact that she was loved and admired by those around her did not go unnoticed by the girl but only seemed to enhance her genuine desire to help others. A good student, she excelled in dance, art, and English and devoted several hours each week to volunteering with her parents at a local homeless shelter. For her thirteenth birthday, she asked that donations be made to the shelter in lieu of personal gifts.

Three months before his niece was to turn fourteen, Victor got what he would later term "The Visit." He was on assignment in South Africa when a fellow agent appeared and told him it was imperative they talk immediately. Sensing that The Visit involved something personal, Victor followed the man to a gleaming apartment building and up to a well-appointed penthouse. It was there that he learned Thomas and Sonia were dead. Their car had gone over the side of an embankment and rolled several times before bursting into flames. The accident had happened during a terrible thunderstorm, and nothing could have been done to save his brother and sister-in-law. His niece hadn't been in the car at the time, and family friends were watching over her.

Within hours, Victor was on a plane bound for Virginia. He'd talked with the authorities, the people who were caring for his niece, and the funeral home. As for Tory, he hadn't yet spoken to her. He didn't know what to say.

Once at his brother's home, Victor thanked the neighbors who'd gathered to offer condolences and provide comfort to Thomas and Sonia Jones's young daughter. After a brief conversation with the husband and wife who'd been staying with Tory, Victor walked to the girl's room and stood at the door. What should he tell her? What should he do?

He found his niece sitting on the floor beside her bed. Her knees were pulled up in front of her, and her shoulder-length brown hair was pulled back into a ponytail. It was obvious that she'd been crying, but her cheeks were now dry. In her arms, she held a fuzzy brown rabbit he'd given her for Easter one year.

Lowering himself next to her, Victor said the first words that came to mind.

"I wish I could have gotten here sooner."

Leaning against him, she said, "Me, too."

Putting an arm around her shoulders, he asked, "Is there anything I can do to make it better?"

"No, but thank you for asking."

They sat without speaking for a long time. Eventually, Tory fell asleep in his arms. As Victor stared down at the girl, he thought of the early years when holding this sleeping child had given him so much comfort. He found that it gave him comfort now.

Victor moved into his brother's house. He was Tory's only living relative and quickly became her legal guardian. Within weeks, he'd used his connections in The Agency in order to gain a position as an instructor at a regional training facility for covert operatives. For the first time in his life, Victor worked from nine a.m. to five p.m. in a fixed location. He was shocked to find that he actually enjoyed the change.

As Tory started high school, her uncle settled into the routine of juggling work, carpool with other parents for after school activities and club meetings, and attendance at parent-teacher conferences. Again, he was amazed at how smoothly he made the transition from his lonely but exciting former lifestyle to that of devoted, dependable parent. Admittedly, Tory made things extremely easy in this regard. Victor was in awe of how the girl brought joy to everyone despite her own grief regarding the loss of her father and mother.

One December evening, Victor arrived home to find the front door unlocked. The twinkling lights on the Christmas tree shone brightly, but the rest of the house was dark. He withdrew his gun and made a hasty search of the rooms. It appeared that nothing had been disturbed, but his niece was conspicuously absent.

Don't panic, he thought. *Maybe she's at a friend's house. Is there something at her school I forgot about? Perhaps the practice for the Christmas program was today and not tomorrow.*

He acknowledged the absurdity of his attempts at self-placation. His attention to detail had always been one of his most exceptional qualities, and he knew that his recent change in lifestyle had in no way diminished his abilities. Withdrawing his iPhone, he made the call for help to The Agency. His niece's disappearance could not be coincidental. It must have something to do with him.

Silently cursing himself and whoever was responsible for the child's disappearance, Victor slipped out of the back door and instantly noticed that someone had walked through the leaves in the yard. No professional would have left evidence like that unless he wanted Victor to quickly discover it. Hurrying now, Victor followed the path of disturbed leaves and entered the woods of the park behind the house.

He found Tory lying on her back half a mile away. It was obvious from a distance that she was alive and in pain, although she had no visible wounds. Victor glanced around before kneeling beside the girl, but the perpetrator was nowhere in sight. He knew if someone had used his niece to lure him to his death, then it was over. He didn't care. All he cared about was Tory.

He said her name, and she looked up at him with pleading eyes and struggled to speak. Reassuring her that everything would be fine, Victor performed a hasty examination of the girl. Her pulse rate was erratic. He found that her right arm had several bruises on it, and there was a puncture wound near the crease at her elbow. A purple bruise highlighted the injection site.

"Who did this to you?" he demanded. "Was he tall? Short? Blonde? Brunette? Fat? Skinny?"

"N-no, Uncle Victor."

Confused, he repeated, "No? Tory, you have to tell me who did this. I'm going to find him and make him pay for what he did to you."

She moaned then shook her head.

"You…can't."

Her voice was barely audible, but he could hear the conviction behind her words.

"Help will be here any second. You have to tell me before they arrive. That way I can find who did this to you and stop him from doing it to someone else."

"You'll…you'll kill them, you mean."

Victor blinked in surprise.

"I know what you do," his niece said, as she reached for his hand. "Mom and Dad…I knew what they did before they got married. Please, don't. Please, stop. It's not right."

A bullet pierced his chest. The impact knocked him backward. Rolling over, Victor got to his knees then looked down and watched the red stain spread quickly across the front of his shirt.

So, this is how it ends, he thought. *I fail. I let my parents, my brother, my sister-in-law, my country, and most importantly Tory down. After everything I've seen and done, I deserve that. Not Tory. Tory has to live.*

Droplets of his blood fell onto the girl's school sweatshirt as he bent forward to kiss her on the forehead. Her breathing was becoming more shallow, and tears filled his eyes. He'd never felt more helpless in his life.

From somewhere nearby in the woods, he heard a haughty female voice laced with a Hispanic accent taunting, "The Great Victor Jones. You are not quite what I expected, but then I expected more from your brother and his wife as well. You disappoint me."

When the young woman stepped into the clearing, he immediately recognized her. He and Thomas had been the agents responsible for assassinating her parents and destroying their network of heroin trafficking and prostitution. Although only ten at the time, their daughter had sworn to avenge her parents. The Jones brothers had considered her words to be empty threats. After all, how many children had uttered that same statement and not followed through?

In one fluid movement, Victor grabbed his gun, raised his arm, aimed, and fired. The woman staggered back, raised her own gun, and crumpled to the ground.

"Uncle Victor?"

"I didn't aim to kill," he said aloud. "When they find us, they'll find her alive."

The girl smiled slightly and whispered, "You did the right thing. I'm so proud of you."

He watched her eyes close as he collapsed beside her. He heard the movement of agents coming towards them and looked at his niece one last time before allowing himself to succumb to unconsciousness. He was ready to surrender to death and the tantalizing peace it offered him.

Let me die and let Tory live.
"Come on, Mr. Jones. Open your eyes."

The male voice was unfamiliar, but Victor felt compelled to comply with the request. The moment he forced his eyelids apart, he understood that he was in a hospital. The man standing beside his bed was evidently a nurse. Victor had no doubt that he was also an employee of The Agency.

"Good job," the stranger said encouragingly. "I was beginning to wonder if that would ever happen. I've been after you to wake up for the last week."

Victor lay still and silent. He wanted to ask this nurse about Tory but was afraid of the information the man might have about his niece. When he closed his eyes, the stranger protested and ordered him to open them again. Victor ignored him.

"The woman responsible for what happened is dead," the nurse quietly informed him. "Her henchmen are dead, too."

As his eyes snapped open, Victor rasped, "I didn't shoot to kill."

"No, you didn't."

Victor understood in an instant what someone in the responding party had done.

He hadn't killed his would-be assassin, but those in the Agency had seen to it that she was eliminated. He had no doubt that everyone else who'd helped with her plot was also now dead.

"My niece...?" he asked hoarsely.

A long silence followed. Finally, the nurse shook his head and admitted, "She was gone before we reached you. I'm sorry."

TRUE

The man sounded genuinely affected by the passing of the child, and Victor thought, *Even in death, Tory still touches people.*

"...gone back over the evidence left at the crash site where your brother and his wife died," the agent was telling him. "The cause is still undetermined, but we're thinking the car was forced off the road during that storm. This woman had quite a network of goons out there working with her on the revenge plot. It turns out that her grandfather had his own money and was financing...."

Victor closed his eyes and turned his head. He didn't want to hear any more about the woman, the plot, or his family. None of it mattered. All of the people he loved were dead, and nothing would change that. He wished he could join them.

The following week, Victor left the hospital and took a cab to the morgue. He appreciated that his friends in The Agency had arranged for his niece's body to remain there until he'd recovered enough to see her. He knew there would be a funeral. He couldn't deny her neighbors, teachers, and friends their opportunity to say their final goodbyes. However, he wanted a few moments alone with her.

In truth, Victor also wanted to verify that Tory was actually dead. He was too well-trained to believe anything anyone told him. He had to have proof.

He left the morgue convinced and directed the cab driver to take him home. The house was eerily quiet as he wandered through the empty rooms. The gaily decorated Christmas tree mocked him with its brightly-colored ornaments and wrapped presents underneath.

Victor slowly climbed the stairs and went to Tory's room. Sitting on the edge of the mattress, he saw his niece everywhere – in the artwork on the walls, in the framed photographs on her desk, in the books on the shelves, in her comforter and curtains, and in her treasured childhood toys and trinkets. Her favorite sweater was draped over the back of the desk chair, and her brush rested on the nightstand next to a half-full glass of water and a gingerbread cookie that was still sealed in its colorful plastic wrap.

It was the sight of the gingerbread man that broke Victor. Tory would never get to eat it, to enjoy that simple pleasure or any other pleasure ever again. She would never drink the glass of water, brush her hair, read the books, paint any pictures, wear her favorite sweater, look through the curtains, or cover herself with the comforter. She was no more.

Within a month's time, Victor had tendered his resignation from The Agency, sold the house in Virginia, and donated most of its furnishings to the homeless shelter where his niece, brother, and sister-in-law had once volunteered. What belongings remained were put in storage along with his own personal possessions. Taking only what would fit in his SUV, Victor left Virginia with no particular destination in mind.

He drove aimlessly for weeks. When the gas gauge read low, he stopped to fill the tank. When he was hungry, he pulled over at whatever restaurant he happened to notice on the side of the road. When he was tired, he stayed at the first hotel, motel, or truck stop he came upon. One day blended into the next, and Victor moved through his life without purpose for the first time since the deaths of his parents.

The week before Easter, Victor found himself on the West coast of Florida. As he walked along one of the local beaches, he spotted a For Rent sign in the window of a run-down bungalow set back in a tangle of overgrowth. The little house was an incongruous sight, a worn structure in the midst of renovated homes and newly-constructed condos.

Curiosity got the better of Victor, and he walked up to the door of the bungalow and knocked. After a few moments, the door was opened by a brown-eyed, blonde-haired woman who appeared to be in her early thirties. She wore paint-spattered overalls that didn't quite fit, a white tee shirt, and sandals. Her hair had been pulled up and clipped haphazardly behind her head.

"I saw the sign in the window."

The woman smiled and held out a hand streaked with rust-colored paint. Victor didn't hesitate to shake it as he introduced himself.

"I'm Jocelyn Kramer," the woman told him as she ushered him inside. "I inherited this place from my aunt and can't afford the taxes or repair work that has to be done. I need a roommate."

Realizing that he was interested in something for the first time since Tory's death, Victor asked for a tour. Jocelyn led him around the house, which was actually much larger than it appeared from the beach.

"Are you doing all the renovations yourself?" he asked after being shown the room for rent.

"I don't make much working with Special Ed kids. I've been spending a lot of time watching

HGTV and talking to the guys at Home Depot." She brightened suddenly and asked, "Why? Are you in construction?"

He smiled for the first time in months and admitted, "My field is economics." When she looked crestfallen, he added, "I am pretty versatile though. I'm sure I could help with some of the basic repairs and cosmetic work."

Cocking her head, Jocelyn said brightly, "Okay."

Startled, Victor echoed, "Okay? You don't know anything about me."

"I know your name is Victor Jones and that you're an economist who's versatile and wants to rent a room and help me out with the house. What more do I need to know?"

"There's a lot about me that you might not like. You should be careful about renting a room to someone you just met. At least do a background check or something."

Jocelyn grinned and said, "You're asking me to do a background check on you, so I'm assuming I won't find out that you're a serial killer."

Victor stared at the woman for a long moment before muttering, "I should go."

When he turned to leave, Jocelyn stepped forward and placed a hand on his forearm then said, "You look like you need to stay." She paused then insisted, "Stay."

Against his better judgment, Victor stayed. He and Jocelyn worked on the house together during her Easter holiday. When she returned to the classroom, he continued the painting and supervised plumbers and electricians. The decaying house was quickly being brought back to life through his and Jocelyn's efforts. It made Victor feel less aimless and slightly hopeful about the future.

He liked Jocelyn. At thirty-four, she was fourteen years younger than he was and loved her life, her job, her neighbors, and her students. He began to look forward to the time they spent together working on the house, talking, eating dinner, and watching the sunset every day.

"Tell me what you did," Jocelyn said one late May evening as they sat in the beach chairs waiting for the sun's nightly performance.

"I took down the wallpaper in the guest bathroom."

Placing her empty wine glass on the sand beside her chair, Jocelyn said, "That's not what I meant. Tell me what you did before you were here."

"I can't."

"Of course you can."

Victor suddenly realized that he wanted Jocelyn. He'd been physically intimate with many women during his adult life, but he had never been interested in anything except sex. With Jocelyn, he wanted more. It was a shocking revelation that brought with it a host of unexpected challenges.

"If I tell you what I used to do for a living, you'll ask me to leave."

"Never. I love the kind, generous, and wonderful person you are now."

Victor wanted to scoff at her choice of words. Instead, he felt tears sting his eyes and worked hard to swallow the lump in his throat.

"Before last Christmas…."

He couldn't actually tell her about his work at the Agency. If he did, then he would be breaking all the rules and endangering her life. His admission to anyone might also jeopardize other agents in the field and change the outcomes of missions he'd long since successfully completed.

He finally settled on, "I did very bad things for the good of our country."

Jocelyn nodded then asked, "Did your family know?"

"My parents were in the same line of work. They died on the job when I was thirteen. My younger brother and I had been groomed to follow in their footsteps. He and my sister-in-law...retired from the business, but they were killed years later by someone...because of one of our assignments. Last December, I came home and found my niece...my beautiful niece...."

Victor stood abruptly and went into the house. He refused to cry in front of anyone, especially Jocelyn. He had to keep his emotions in check.

Retreating to his room, Victor sat on the edge of the mattress and fought to rein in his desire to cry. Jocelyn rapped lightly on the door then stepped into the room. Victor turned his head away from her and clenched his jaw.

He listened as she walked across the terrazzo tile towards him. She stopped in front of where he sat, and her hands rested on his shoulders before sliding up his neck and into his hair. Her palms moved along the sides of his face, and she gently guided him until he was looking up at her.

"You aren't responsible for your niece's death," she said gently but firmly.

"You don't even know the circumstances."

"I know you. You're a good man, Victor Jones. I think I love you."

He told her he loved her without hesitation. The rush of emotion that accompanied this utterance was unfamiliar and incredibly gratifying. Pulling Jocelyn towards him, he buried his face against her neck then drew her onto the bed beside him.

Victor expected to wake the next morning and find the events of the previous night had been part of a dream. He imagined he'd open his eyes and see that he was alone in the bed. As he lifted his eyelids, he steeled himself against the inevitable.

Jocelyn was nowhere in the room. Disheartened, Victor silently berated himself for considering the notion that he was worthy of love from any woman, much less a woman like Jocelyn. He was nothing more than an assassin who'd gotten what he deserved when his family had been taken from him.

"Good morning, sleepyhead. I was beginning to worry that you wouldn't wake up in time."

Jocelyn stood in the doorway of his room wearing faded pajamas and holding a tray filled with two mugs and a plate of muffins. As Victor slowly sat up in the bed, he began, "Last night –"

Her face fell, and she said, "Please don't tell me you thought it was a mistake. I couldn't handle it if you said you changed your mind about loving me."

Relieved that his dream was actually reality, Victor hastened to reassure her that his feelings for her hadn't changed. She beamed at him and carried the tray over to the bed then lowered it onto the comforter before carefully leaning across it to kiss him.

"I wish we had more time," she murmured. "If I don't eat and shower soon, then I'll be late."

"Late for what?"

"School. It's Monday, remember? I'm taking the students to the natural history museum for a field trip." Sighing, she admitted, "It's going to be a challenge. We don't have as many people as usual available to help with the kids."

Before he realized what he was saying, Victor offered, "I could help."

"I think I'm definitely going to be a little late for work," she declared, as she moved the tray to the nightstand and wrapped her arms around his neck. "Okay, maybe I'll miss all of Assembly...."

Later that morning, Victor stood in the museum surrounded by special needs children. He was in awe of these middle school boys and girls and of the way Jocelyn interacted with them.

"Mr. Teacher's Helper!" called out a boy with Down's Syndrome. "Look at what I did!"

Victor smiled and walked over to the child, who was proudly pointing to a completed puzzle that depicted manatees feasting on underwater vegetation. He applauded the successful effort and was surprised when the boy thanked him both with words and a hug. He hesitantly hugged back and was rewarded with a similar feeling to the one he'd experienced when he'd hugged his young niece. It wasn't the same as holding Tory, but the warmth and connection to the goodness in life was definitely there.

TRUE

He scanned the activities room and spotted Jocelyn standing beside a child with cerebral palsy. The girl, who appeared to be around twelve, was in a motorized wheelchair and utilized a computer in order to communicate with those around her. From an early age, Victor had unapologetically pondered what purpose the existence of such individuals could possibly serve. Even now, he wondered whether or not it would have been better if the child in the wheelchair had died at birth. She could only move one arm and hand, and her speech was unintelligible. What kind of life was that?

As if she were reading his mind, Jocelyn hailed Victor from across the room. When he came to stand beside her, she suggested that perhaps he could discuss economics with the child while she went to guide an autistic girl to the bathroom.

Victor found himself confused. Jocelyn seemed an unlikely person to be cruel to anyone, much less a special needs child. Why would she suggest he engage in a conversation about economics with someone so young and so challenged?

He thought of his niece and of how accepting she'd been of every person she'd met. If there was one thing he could do that would truly honor her memory, then it was to follow in her footsteps and make an attempt at redemption.

After introducing himself, Victor told the girl he'd graduated with a degree in economics twenty-five years earlier and had gone on to earn his Master's degree a year later. The girl absorbed this information then quickly moved her hand across the keyboard in front of her. Soon, a synthesized voice emanated from the speakers and said, "My name is Melody. I want to get my Ph.D. in economics. What are your thoughts on Keynes' theories and his anti-classical economic movement against such economists as David Ricardo?"

Stunned by the child's involved question, Victor debated economic philosophies and practices with Melody for the following hour. By the time they ended their dialogue, he had all but forgotten about her twisted limbs, her inability to communicate save for the synthesizer, and her youth. Her intellect was formidable, and he had no doubt that she would one day earn her Ph.D. and most likely become one of the leading economists of her time.

"What did you think?" Jocelyn asked Victor that night as they watched the sun setting over the water.

"About what?"

"The field trip."

"I enjoyed it."

"And your talk with Melody?"

"It was humbling."

"She's brilliant, isn't she?"

"Yes. She told me that her body might keep her trapped in her wheelchair, but her mind was always free. Talking with her was extremely gratifying. Thank you."

Jocelyn smiled and said, "You're welcome. Maybe you could talk to her again. You could be her mentor."

"And she could be mine, kind of like Tory used to be, kind of like you are now." As he watched the waves rolling in and out, he admitted, "Until I came here I thought Tory was the only person who could help me to open my heart. I realize now that I was wrong."

"You were. *You* are the only person who can open your heart," Jocelyn offered.

Victor considered this as the fiery ball in the sky sank towards the horizon. When darkness finally fell, he looked down into his still-full wine glass and said, "I'd like to stay with you, get married and maybe have a couple of kids. Does that sound crazy?"

"Not to me."

"My heart tells me that I belong here."

For the first time in his life, Victor didn't hesitate to follow his heart. It was the right thing to do, and he was ready to go wherever it might lead him.

Imagine

The way Emma Jen looked at it, the course of her life had been determined the moment she'd been given her name. Her mother and father were free-spirited lackadaisical people who couldn't keep track of their own lives much less that of a child. According to her uncle, her parents had initially decided not to name their new baby girl and were going to let her select a name for herself once she could speak. However, pressure from more conservative family and friends had finally worn them down, and they'd announced at a Christmas party that their daughter's name was Imagine. This caused quite a stir at the holiday gathering, and distressed grandparents' pleas for something more traditional had won out in the end. Emma Jen had been the compromise.

And compromise had been the recurrent theme throughout Emma Jen's forty-seven years. She was a red-haired, blue eyed beauty with above average intelligence and a quick wit. As a child, she'd imagined there could be structure in her parents' chaotic world, so she'd been the one to clean and organize the house. Her mother, a smart, talented folk singer who worked for a variety of local restaurants as a waitress, couldn't keep track of her schedule, find her purse, or take the time away from her own interests to be involved in her daughter's activities at school or at home. Emma Jen's father was a handyman who dreamed of being an actor and spent most of his time after work volunteering at the theater either participating in productions or drinking with his friends. Neither of her parents was home much.

When she graduated from high school, Emma Jen imagined going away from her Mississippi hometown to college in New York or California, but lack of family funds had forced her to attend the local community college. Her dream of becoming a buyer for upscale department stores had been exchanged for a managerial position at the local warehouse store. Her desire to marry a handsome man with a great sense of humor who was also romantic had been pushed aside when she'd accepted the proposal of a nice, ordinary-looking guy who worked hard but never thought to surprise her with flowers or an evening out. Emma Jen longed for one child and her husband wanted three so they compromised and had two. When her husband died unexpectedly at thirty of an aneurysm, Emma Jen struggled but did her best to raise their two children on her own while continuing to work full-time. Two decades passed after her husband's untimely death, but nothing much seemed to change for Emma Jen.

With her forty-eighth birthday approaching, Emma Jen was tired of compromise. She wasn't getting any younger, and she wasn't certain if she was gaining any wisdom as she advanced in years. Her son, David, and daughter, Ann, were like carbon copies of Emma Jen's parents and could never seem to find their cell phones, mail, car keys, or steady jobs. Ann and her wild red-headed, blue-eyed three year-old daughter, E.J., had recently moved in with Emma Jen after Ann's divorce from a frequently unemployed construction worker, and David had never left home.

"You have to get jobs," was Emma Jen's daily pronouncement. "I don't earn enough money to support the four of us. Ann, you've got five years of experience total as a cashier. David, your degree is in computer science, so use it! You two need to either find work or go back to school."

"Times are tough, Mom," Ann insisted. "Cashier jobs just aren't there."

"Let's assume for a minute that what you're saying is true. You have a child to care for, so you take a job cleaning toilets if it's the only way you can provide for her." Turning to David, she said, "And you can't tell me there are no computer jobs around."

"There aren't," he declared petulantly. "Lori was lucky to find the one she has."

Lori was David's girlfriend. She had a degree in computer science as well and was employed by a large electronics store. She worked a forty hour week and gave a lot of her money to David even though Emma Jen couldn't understand why. He didn't seem to do anything with the money except buy cigarettes and video games.

"Move in with Lori then," Emma Jen told David. "I love you, but you're twenty-four now. You need to be on your own and learn what it's like to be a man."

So, David moved out, and Emma Jen only had herself, Ann, and E.J. to support. Ann slept late every day, while Emma Jen went to work and E.J. played unsupervised. The house was a wreck with dirty clothes on the floor, dirty dishes in the sink, and toys strewn all over the place.

One night, Emma Jen returned home from work to find Ann watching television while E.J. colored all over one wall. The house was a mess, as usual.

"E.J. is going to daycare, and you're going to work!" Emma Jen announced angrily. "What happened to you, Ann? Where is your head? You have responsibilities!"

"I never asked for them," Ann replied nonchalantly. "You were always so wrapped up in your job that you didn't have time for us."

Mortified, Emma Jen countered, "I never imagined my life would turn out like this! I worked hard at something I didn't want to do to make sure we had a roof over our heads, clothes on our backs, and food in our stomachs! That didn't leave much time for anything else! I had two children to raise by myself. Why is it so difficult for you to understand? That's what you *do*! You work hard and provide security for your family!"

"That may be what *you* do, but it's not what I want to do."

"You have a child to think of."

"You'll take care of her," Ann snapped. "Obviously, you think you did a great job with me and David, so you can do just as well with E.J. I'm leaving."

Emma Jen watched in disbelief as Ann left the house. She turned to look at E.J., who'd stopped coloring on the wall and appeared as though she might cry. Emma Jen went over to her granddaughter and lifted her up then brought her to the kitchen. She fed the child a bowl of macaroni and cheese then read her a story before bathing her and putting her to bed.

TRUE

Then she went to her own room, sat on the mattress, and cried.

"Where did I go wrong?" she asked herself. "I've tried so hard all my life to do the right thing despite what I wanted, and look where I am. My parents and my children are so scatter-brained that they'd lose their heads if they weren't attached to their bodies. My husband's been dead for almost twenty years. I hate my job, and now I'm alone with E.J. I can't do it again! I can't raise another child on my own, especially not now. What happened to my dreams and hopes for the future?"

There was a light knock on Emma Jen's bedroom door. She wiped away her tears with a tissue then called for E.J. to enter. The child padded over to her and asked where her mother was.

"I don't know," Emma Jen said truthfully. "I think it's going to be just you and me from now on."

The little girl looked pensive for a while then asked, "Grandma, can I sleep with you tonight?"

"Of course you can."

"What about when you go to work tomorrow?"

"I'm not going to work tomorrow. You and I have things to do."

The following morning, Emma Jen took E.J. with her to the courthouse and petitioned for custody of her granddaughter. Then they went to several daycares, and E.J. was soon registered at the one both of them liked the most. By dinnertime that evening, the house was clean, and E.J. had helped her grandmother to scrub the crayon marks off the wall. The little girl seemed happier and calmer than she had since she'd been an infant.

Ann did not return. Since no one knew where the child's father was, Emma Jen was eventually granted sole custody of E.J. David and his girlfriend moved away, and Emma Jen settled into a new routine. Everything revolved around E.J. and their life together. For the first time in years, Emma Jen was happy. She'd taken a stand and could live with the harsh reality of her children's reactions. She hoped one day that they'd come back to her and be well-adjusted, responsible adults. If that didn't happen, then she would have to accept it and keep moving forward.

Two years passed. When it came time for E.J.'s graduation from kindergarten, Emma Jen dressed the child in her most adorable outfit and took the day off from work. She arrived at the school wearing her Sunday best and carrying a camera to take pictures of the momentous event. She hurried to find a seat in the front row and prepared for the ceremony to begin.

"Which one's yours?" someone asked from beside her.

Emma Jen turned and saw a man about her age. He had some gray interwoven throughout his brown hair, but he was in great shape and had a nice smile and beautiful brown eyes.

"Her name's E.J."

"Oh, E.J.," he said knowingly. "My grandson, Leo, can't stop talking about E.J. and how they like to play kickball at recess. I think he has a crush on her. He told me she has pretty red hair and bright blue eyes. Now I know where she got them."

Emma Jen smiled and said, "She's mentioned Leo every day since kindergarten started. I think she has a crush on him, too." Glancing around the man, she asked, "Are Leo's parents here? I'd love to meet them."

"I'm Leo's parent. Well, I'm really his grandfather, but I have guardianship of him. My son and his wife got into drugs when Leo was a baby, and my wife and I took him in. She died of breast cancer a year later, and I've raised him alone ever since."

"Oh, I'm so sorry. I'm E.J.'s grandmother, and I'm raising her myself. Her mother...." Emma Jen's voice trailed off, and she eventually said, "I don't know where I went wrong. I raised both of my kids by myself after their father died, and they just never quite *got* it if you know what I mean."

The man nodded with understanding and said, "I'm Bill."

"Emma Jen. E.J.'s named after me."

"Emma Jen. That's a lovely and unusual name."

"It stands for Imagine, if you can believe that. The irony of it is that I think I gave up on imagining when I was about E.J.'s age." Looking up towards the stage as the kindergarteners filed in, she added, "I don't want that to happen to her. She needs to dream and keep dreaming but be focused on her goals."

"Sounds like she's lucky to have you," Bill remarked. "Say, why don't we all go for ice cream to celebrate once this is over? I've taken the day off from work and think maybe we should all get to know each other a little better."

"What do you do for a living?"

"I manage a local restaurant. I always wanted to own a chain of Italian restaurants, but my family didn't have the money to send me to college. So, I started out as a dishwasher and worked my way up the ladder, so to speak. I still wish I'd gone to college, but I do okay for myself and Leo."

Emma Jen smiled and said, "I think we have a lot in common. Perhaps you and I can have dinner sometime soon and really talk."

Bill smiled back and said, "I'd like that very much."

Two days later, a deliveryman from a local florist appeared at Emma Jen's store with a bouquet of roses for her. The card read, "Imagine me and you. – Bill"

The following week, Emma Jen and Bill hired a babysitter and went out to dinner at a nice restaurant located downtown near the river. Emma Jen hadn't been on a date in almost thirty years and found that she was nervous and excited. Bill confided to her that he was in the same predicament, and they laughed and spent the evening talking of their lives, their pasts, and their dreams. Bill took Emma Jen out dancing after dinner and kissed her as they stood on the doorstep to her house before they went inside to pay the babysitter. They agreed to start having "Date Night" once a week. That way, they had an evening out and the children had a play date.

About three months into their relationship, Emma Jen and Bill talked each other into going back to school. They were both fifty, couldn't afford to quit their jobs, and had two young children to raise. Although they questioned their sanity, they decided to forge ahead and follow their dream of furthering their education.

"We may be the oldest people ever to graduate by the time this is done," Emma Jen muttered, as she filled out the college application. "I don't even know if they'll accept my Associate's degree, since I got it so long ago."

"At least you have some experience with college," Bill reminded her. "It's all new to me."

"You're a smart, handsome man. You're going to do fine."

"And you're a beautiful, intelligent woman who is going to wow everyone in her classes."

Emma Jen blushed and directed her attention to the paperwork she was filling out. An idea suddenly popped into her head, and she couldn't seem to make it go away. After a while, she quit trying and lowered the pen in her hand to the table and looked up at Bill, who eyed her suspiciously.

"What are you thinking? Should I be afraid?"

She laughed and admitted, "Maybe. I was thinking that I love you and maybe I should ask you to marry me. I've spent my whole life compromising myself to please others – my parents, my husband, my children, my bosses, and society in general. I swore I wasn't going to do that anymore when I got custody of E.J. I want her to see that women don't have to lose their own identity when they take on what challenges life has in store for them. You get that, and I love you for it. You appreciate me for everything I am and don't ask me to change. I hope you know that I appreciate the man you are."

"Imagine me and you," Bill said with a broad smile. "Or should I say Emma Jen, me, and two? After all, it would be you, me, E.J., and Leo. Are you ready for that?"

"I'm ready for anything," Emma Jen declared. "No compromises and no turning back. I can imagine anything and make it my reality. It's about time. It's nice to finally be me."

TRUE

CHECK OUT BARBARA CUTRERA'S PUBLISHED AND UPCOMING RELEASES & STAY CONNECTED

Explore other published works by the author at www.amazon.com, www.barnesandnoble.com and www.goodreads.com.

"Like" Barbara Cutrera and become a fan by going to the *Barbara Cutrera, Author* Facebook Page.

Visit Barbara Cutrera's website at www.onmywayuponline.com to read her blog, learn about her other works, view links, and find out more about the author.

This book is also available in electronic format at most online retailers

About the Author

Barbara Cutrera has been a writer since childhood but didn't begin writing novels until 1999. She decided to pursue publication in 2012. Cutrera is an author who likes to write in various genres – fiction, mystery, contemporary romance, fantasy romance, and romantic suspense.

A member of the Romance Writers of America, the Florida Writers' Association, and the Tampa Area Romance Authors, Cutrera was born and raised in Louisiana and moved to Florida with her family in 2004. She works with the visually-impaired and is visually-impaired herself. She believes that our minds are only limited by the restrictions we place upon them. Her literary credo? "Transcending reality by exploring it one story at a time...."

In a Manner of Speaking

This mystery was the first novel published by Barbara Cutrera (July, 2012). It is available in print and electronic format.

    Neile Landry, a talented corporate interpreter, is forced to face her past fears and rethink her future plans as she is confronted with deception, threats to her life, and murder. When Neile's wealthy employer dies in a suspicious car accident that also critically injures her co-worker and best friend, she forms an unlikely partnership with Scotsman Ewen Erskine, a recent business acquaintance. Erskine suddenly inherits his uncle's multinational corporation after the older man's unexpected death on the same night as the mysterious demise of Neile's boss. As secret plans for a global healthcare network are revealed, more deaths follow.
    Neile soon finds herself in a personal as well as professional relationship with Erskine as they work together in their efforts to uncover the truth about those who have fallen prey to foul play. Their journey takes them from Louisiana to Scotland, but the killer follows.
    As they grapple with personal threats and insidious attacks by an elusive sociopath, Neile struggles to overcome increasing difficulty with a congenital cardiac condition and her painful past, while Erskine tries to deal with terrible secrets from

his youth that have troubled him most of his life. In the terrifying inevitable confrontation with the killer, Neile realizes that more is at stake than she ever imagined. If the murderer prevails, then everyone she cares about, including innocent children, will die. Neile Landry will have to do whatever she must in order to stop a sociopath bent on the destruction of all she holds dear even if she is forced to forfeit her own life in the process.

Over, Under, Across & Through
Book 1 of The Real World Series

This first book in the author's fiction series was published in December, 2012. It is available in print and electronic format.

    A young widower fights to overcome substance abuse and emotional instability as his daughter attempts to find solace for them despite overwhelming odds. Set in southern Louisiana, *Over, Under, Across & Through* tells the story of Tristan and Sarah Maes and their extended family. The novel is divided into three parts. Each part highlights a different time period in their lives during the 1970s, 1980s and 1990s and explores how the father and daughter and those closest to them confront abuse, neglect, and deception.

    While Tristan grapples with the loss of his wife and the subsequent battle with alcohol and drugs, Sarah strives to carve out a normal life for herself. This is made more difficult by the onset of juvenile macular degeneration, which results in partial blindness that develops during her teenaged years. Parent and child must come to grips with their actions and choices in the past in order to gain the elusive peace of mind so desperately sought by both in their present.

The Healer's Gift

This romantic fantasy was published in September of 2013. It is available in print and electronic format and available in audio format.

Ainsland, a virgin widow fleeing from her husband's murderer, and Collum, a healer who possesses supernatural abilities, are brought together by circumstance. What begins as a marriage of convenience for the couple evolves into one of great love and passion. Yet, Collum's tragic past and the ever-looming threat of Ainsland's malevolent pursuer's appearance in their close-knit rural community overshadow their ability to be truly content. When evil strikes and all seems lost, will it be the resilient, headstrong Ainsland who is able to save herself, her husband, and the people she has come to know and cherish or will Collum, determined and wise, somehow manage to rescue the love of his life before time runs out?

TRUE

A Good Man's Life
Book 2 of The Real World Series

The second book in the author's fiction series published in February, 2014. It is available in print and electronic format.

Daniel Nash struggles to reconcile his feelings of betrayal with his desire to understand his life. His hopes of uncovering the secrets revealed in his father's journals are quickly dashed, and he works with a private investigator to discover the truth. Worry about his wife, Sarah, combines with his efforts to cope with his childhood trauma, an unexpected death, and the recent revelations. His obsession with the past threatens to destroy his stable life. Meanwhile, Sarah and her father, Tristan, continue to combat the lingering discord that developed between them years before but refuse to take their main focus from Daniel. As he reviews his biological father's efforts to be a good man, Daniel searches for a way to comprehend shocking disclosures. He questions his own goodness as he fights not to emotionally withdraw from those around him, especially Sarah and Tristan, the two people he knows will always love him.

Future releases by Barbara Cutrera include:

- ***Mercy*** - Book 3 of The Real World Series
- ***Prim and Proper***
- ***Compromising Positions***
- *A Lovely Dream*
- *A Lovely Reality*
- *Lucky*
- *Sight Unseen*
- *Jordan's Way*
- *Bound by Grace*

Made in the USA
San Bernardino, CA
25 February 2014